F is for Fiddlehead

A New Brunswick Alphabet

Written by Marilyn Lohnes and Illustrated by Susan Tooke

I would like to thank:

- The community of Metepenagiag, Elder Bertha Augustine, and Ethan, Joe and Katie Augustine. (E)
- Wayne Kerr
- Cheryl Hewitt, Ganong Bros. Limited (G)
- Lisa Savidant, Irving Oil Limited. (I)
- Pierrette Robichaud, Head Heritage Interpreter, Kouchibouguac National Park (J,K)
- Kelly Ross, Curator/Exhibits Director, New Brunswick Sports Hall of Fame. (O)
- Debbie Branch, Xstrata Zinc Canada, Brunswick Mine. (Z)
- Ashley Watson, the Fibre Arts Studio of the New Brunswick College of Craft and Design.
- Photo reference for letters A, B, D, F, H, K, L, M, N, P, Q, S, V, W, and X were used with permission from New Brunswick Tourism and Parks, Canada.

—Susan Tooke

Sleeping Bear Press™

310 North Main Street, Suite 300
Chelsea, MI 48118
www.sleepingbearpress.com

© 2007 Sleeping Bear Press is an imprint of The Gale Group, Inc.

Printed and bound in China.

First Edition

10 9 8 7 6 5 4 3 2 1

Library of Congress Cataloging-in-Publication Data

Lohnes, Marilyn, 1963-
F is for fiddlehead : a New Brunswick alphabet / written by Marilyn Lohnes; illustrated by Susan Tooke.
p. cm.
Summary: "Using the alphabet from A to Z readers can explore exciting topics related to New Brunswick. Provincial symbols, geography, famous people, and natural wonders are featured using simple rhymes and detailed expository text"—Provided by publisher.
ISBN 978-1-58536-318-6
1. New Brunswick—Juvenile literature. 2. English language—Alphabet—Juvenile literature. 3. Alphabet books—Juvenile literature. I. Tooke, Susan. II. Title.

F1042.4.L64 2007
971.5'1—dc22   2007006609

Aa

New Brunswick, or Nouveau-Brunswick, is the only officially bilingual province in Canada. About 33% of the people speak French as their first language. Acadians are the French-speaking descendants of the first European settlers. Acadian settlers were caught in the struggle for power between the French and British. In 1713 France lost most of its Acadian land to Britain in the Treaty of Utrecht. When war broke out again the British, fearing that the Acadians would side with the French, expelled them from the colony. In 1755 thousands of Acadians were deported to England or to British colonies. Some went to present-day Louisiana, where they helped to create the "Cajun" culture (taken from the word "Acadian"). Years later some of them returned, and now live mainly in the northern and eastern regions of the province, the largest area known as the Acadian Peninsula. Acadians celebrate and share their heritage through festivals and events. They have their own flag (blue, white, and red with a yellow star) and anthem, which were chosen at the Acadian convention of 1884.

A is Acadian, strong and true bred
porting the colours of blue, white, and red.
To early French settlers, their customs were dear.
Acadian culture is still present here.

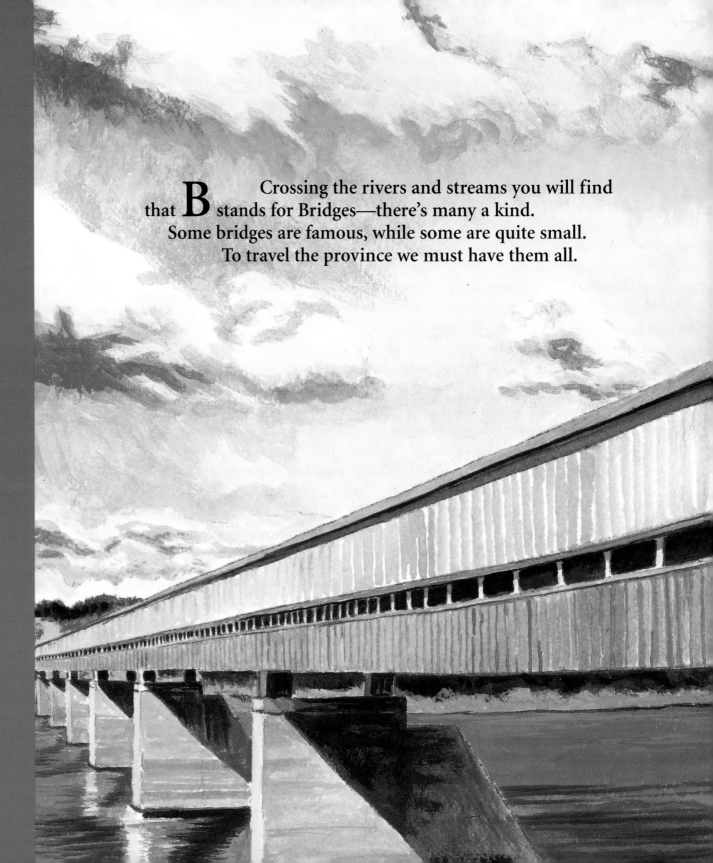

At nearly 391 metres in length, the bridge in Hartland is the longest covered bridge in the world. Its concept began in 1899 when the Hartland Bridge Company was formed by citizens on both sides of the Saint John River. The bridge was officially opened on July 4, 1901. Originally it was a toll bridge with fares of 3 cents for pedestrians, 6 cents for a horse and wagon, and 12 cents for a double team. The tolls were removed when it was purchased by the government of New Brunswick in 1906. It was later recognized for its historical value, and it was declared a national historic site on September 15, 1999.

The shortest covered bridge in New Brunswick crosses the Quisibis River at Rivière-Verte. It is roughly 17 metres long. Another famous bridge is the Confederation Bridge, linking Prince Edward Island to New Brunswick.

B b

Crossing the rivers and streams you will find that B stands for Bridges—there's many a kind. Some bridges are famous, while some are quite small. To travel the province we must have them all.

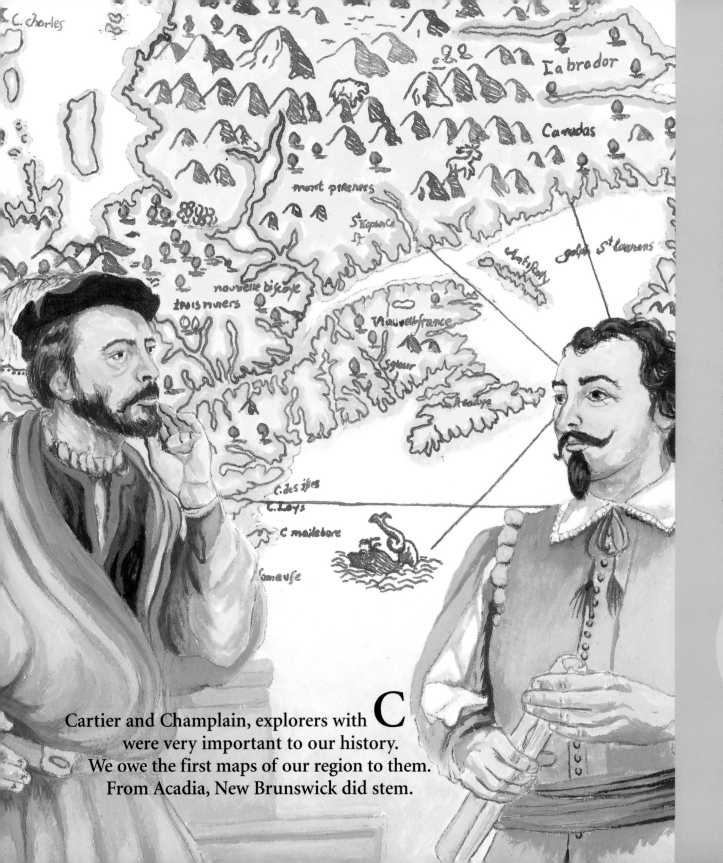

Although Vikings may have been the first to see New Brunswick from their longboats, Jacques Cartier was the first European explorer known to have landed there. He was attempting to find a passage through North America to Asia when he arrived on the northern shore of New Brunswick in the summer of 1534. In 1603 the King of France sent Samuel de Champlain and Pierre du Gua de Monts to the Maritimes to begin settling the region. They landed at the mouth of the Saint Croix River on June 14, 1604. The crew spent a harsh winter on St. Croix Island in Passamaquoddy Bay, where many died. Those who survived moved on to establish a settlement in Nova Scotia in 1605.

Cartographers drew the first maps of this new territory around the time of these explorations. Boundaries were not clearly defined, and land claims included New Brunswick, Nova Scotia, and parts of Maine and Prince Edward Island. Borders crossed hands many times before today's provincial and national borders were established.

Cartier and Champlain, explorers with C
were very important to our history.
We owe the first maps of our region to them.
From Acadia, New Brunswick did stem.

D is for Dulse, or seaweed—it's true.
Some folks in New Brunswick quite like it to chew.
It's picked from the bay when the low tide comes back,
then after it's dried it becomes a good snack.

For some, dulse is a New Brunswick favourite. It is a seaweed that grows mainly in the Bay of Fundy off the New Brunswick coast. When the tide is low, long strands of this seaweed that have been washed up on shore and on rocks are picked by hand. They are then dried in the sun and packaged for local markets. Dulse is also shipped to markets all over North America. It is eaten much like potato chips, as a crisp, salty snack. It can also be pickled and used as a relish.

Long before European settlers arrived in New Brunswick, the land was inhabited by two groups of First Nations peoples—the Mi'kmaq and the Maliseet. The Mi'kmaq settled along northern and eastern New Brunswick coasts. Their name is thought to mean "Kin-friends." Although permanently settled, they migrated into the forests to hunt deer during the winter when fishing was more difficult. The Mi'kmaq culture was strong, emphasizing painting, music, stitchery, fine beadwork, and quillwork. The Maliseet lived west of the Mi'kmaq along the Saint John River. They referred to themselves as "Wolastoqewiyik" (people of the good river). Also talented crafts-people, they were known for their woven baskets and their decorated birch-bark canoes. The two groups spoke similar Algonquian languages that can still be heard today.

There are 15 First Nations communities in New Brunswick—6 Maliseet and 9 Mi'kmaq. Artisans recount legends and create traditional crafts, keeping alive the strong heritage.

E's the esteemed Elder, knowing and wise,
recounting stories 'midst children's wide eyes.
Mi'kmaq and Maliseet live on this land;
their legends were born long before the white man.

F is for Fiddlehead, with rounded head,
growing near streams or along river bed.
The market in Fredericton sells this spring treat.
With butter and lemon, they're tasty to eat.

Ff

Fiddleheads are the coiled leaves of the Ostrich Fern that grows along rivers and streams. In the spring, people can be seen lining up for them at market stalls and roadside stands. Fredericton, Moncton, and Saint John have large markets that sell many interesting New Brunswick products, including fiddleheads. Fiddleheads are also frozen and packaged for sale across Canada.

Fredericton, New Brunswick's capital city, is an important source of culture, art, and education for the province. Along with Moncton, Canada's first officially bilingual city, and Saint John, Canada's oldest incorporated city, it is one of the main urban centres in southern New Brunswick.

Many fine cultural opportunities await you in Fredericton. Famous paintings are found at the Beaverbrook Gallery, New Brunswick's provincial art gallery. The city hosts an annual Harvest Jazz and Blues Festival, as well as a Highland Games event. In the summer visitors can watch the "changing of the guard" in the Historic Garrison District. Other attractions include kayak adventures, friendly cafés, and fine museums.

The town of St. Stephen is home to Canada's oldest candy company, Ganong Bros. Limited. Founded in 1873 by brothers James and Gilbert, it created several firsts in the candy-making industry. In 1885 it invented the chicken bone, a cinnamon flavoured pink candy with a chocolate centre. In 1895 it created Canada's first lollipops, mounted on wooden skewers. Ganong Bros. invented and introduced the first 5-cent chocolate bar in North America—the Pal-O-Mine, in 1910, and in 1932 the company was the first in Canada to sell Valentine chocolates in heart-shaped boxes.

Every year in early August, St. Stephen hosts a week-long Chocolate Festival. The museum details the rich history of Ganong and the chocolate-making industry, while guided tours of the factory demonstrate candy-making procedures.

In 1999 Ganong was named one of Canada's "50 Best Managed Private Companies."

A tastier G could never be found
where candies and chocolate are sold by the pound.
All sorts of treats you are certain to see
if you by chance visit Ganong factory.

g
G

Along the Saint John River King's Landing hides.
To the north Village Acadien can be spied.
The H is for Historic Village—come see!
Within them you'll relive our own history.

Along the south shore of the Saint John River near Fredericton lies the Kings Landing Historical Settlement. A cluster of homes dating from the early to the late 1800s comprises the village. Costumed residents recreate the daily lives of New Brunswick Loyalists—spinning wool, growing herbs, and making soap and butter. Farm animals and gardens are cared for as well. A working saw mill and blacksmith shop are at the heart of the village, along with a mercantile, a church, and the Kings Head Inn.

On the north shore of the Acadian peninsula, is the Village Historique Acadien at Caraquet—an early nineteenth century village. The culture is brought to life through song, dance, and Acadian cuisine. Robin's shed at the village has costumed residents mending nets and drying fish. It represents the fishing shed of Charles Robin, who employed Acadians returning from exile. A lobster hatchery, a tinsmith shop, and the Château Albert Hotel fully complement the village.

Ii

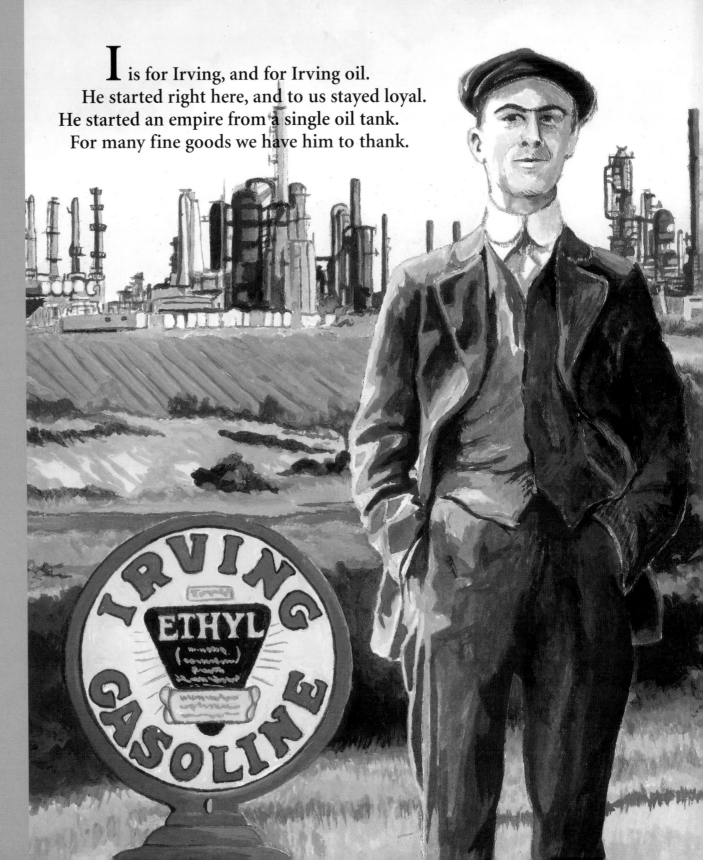

I is for Irving, and for Irving oil.
He started right here, and to us stayed loyal.
He started an empire from a single oil tank.
For many fine goods we have him to thank.

Kenneth Colin Irving built an enormous and diverse business empire. Born in Bouctouche in 1899, he grew from selling Model T Fords and gasoline to becoming the owner of a service station chain and 300 additional companies. Today, more than a decade after his death (1992), the Irving group of companies continues to contribute hundreds of millions of dollars to New Brunswick's economy. Irving is best known for its petroleum processing and service stations, and the Irving oil refinery in Saint John is the largest in Canada. The Irving group of companies also includes pulp and paper mills, trucking lines, forestry, shipbuilding, and media holdings.

The Irving Nature Park, opened in 1992, is a 243-hectare site along the Fundy Coast near Saint John. Schoolchildren from all across the Maritimes visit to see salt marshes, mud flats, high tides, a peninsula of volcanic rock, harbour seals, and more than 250 species of birds. It is one of New Brunswick's richest marine ecosystems. Park staff recount myths and legends, and provide special nature crafts for visitors.

The jellyfish is an unusual creature. It consists of a "bell," made up of a watery gelatinous substance with tentacles and oral arms that look like flaps. The bell is called a medusa, symbolic of the Medusa of Greek mythology with writhing snakes in her hair. The jellyfish has no heart, no bones, no eyes, and no brain, and yet it functions remarkably well as a sea creature. When not floating with the tides it moves through a process similar to jet propulsion. Special muscles on the underside push water out of the hollow bell. As water is pushed in one direction, the jellyfish moves in the opposite direction.

Since most fossils are of animal bones or shells, fossils of jellyfish are a rare find. New Brunswick is one of two known sites that boast the existence of jellyfish fossils (the other being Wisconsin, USA).

J j

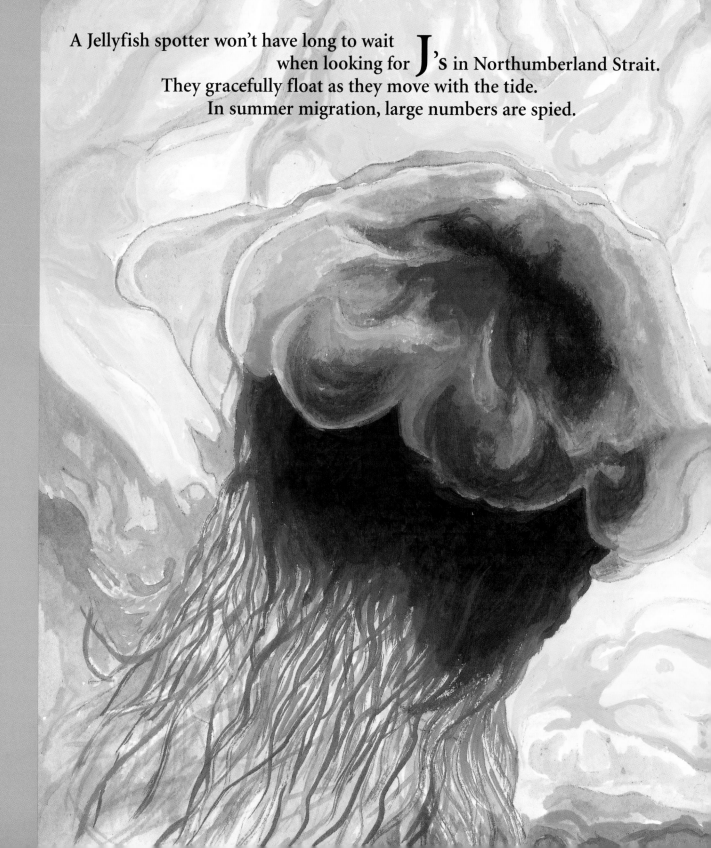

A Jellyfish spotter won't have long to wait
when looking for J's in Northumberland Strait.
They gracefully float as they move with the tide.
In summer migration, large numbers are spied.

Kouchibouguac is our word with a K—
a fine place to visit on a summer day.
Promenade on the boardwalk, or stroll in the sand.
The breeze is delightful, the scenery—grand.

Kouchibouguac National Park is the largest of two national parks in New Brunswick (the other being Fundy National Park), encompassing about 240 square kilometres of wilderness. Running along the Northumberland Strait, it is composed of sandbars, offshore dunes, and long, beautiful beaches with warm lagoon waters.

Boardwalks throughout the park protect the sand dunes and the marsh grasses where varieties of birds come to nest. The lagoons, salt marshes, and peat bogs around the dunes are one of the most productive ecosystems in the world.

Fundy National Park hugs the edge of the Bay of Fundy. Forests and streams blend with rugged coastlines, powerful tides, and rising cliffs of the green Caledonia Highlands. Early residents of the area referred to themselves as the "people of the salt and the fir," describing the salt sea water and air, and the heavily forested area.

L1

Lighthouses are symbols of both the dangers of the waters and the Maritime way.

Travellers were beckoned to a safe landing by some of these historic lighthouses. In 1791 our first lighthouse was built on Partridge Island, near Saint John, where Canada's first immigration quarantine station was established.

New Brunswick still has close to 70 authentic lighthouses, and around 20 replicas. The only staffed lighthouse left in the Maritimes is the Machais Seal Island Lighthouse, off the south-west coast of Grand Manan. It is 18.3 metres tall and wears the typical colors of white with a red cap. The light from it can be seen for over 27 kilometres.

New Brunswicker Robert Foulis invented the world's first steam-powered fog alarm to help guide ships away from rocky shorelines during heavy fog. It was installed in 1859 on Partridge Island. In 1925, nearly 60 years after his death, the Historic Sites and Monuments Board of Canada recognized his contribution and installed a commemorative plaque on the island.

L's for the Lighthouse on rough, rugged cliffs
guarding the coastline and guiding the ships.
The white tower buildings with blazing bright lights
guided the sailors on dark, stormy nights.

M's for Mount Carleton, high in the sky.
Hike it, or bike it, or simply drive by,
With lakes and rivers, you can kayak too.
Enjoy the wildlife, and take in the view.

In 1899 W. F. Ganong identified the highest elevation in New Brunswick and named it Mount Carleton in honour of Thomas Carleton, the first Lieutenant-Governor of New Brunswick. At approximately 820 metres, it is the highest mountain in the Maritime Provinces. On a clear day you can see over 10 million trees from its peak. Mount Carleton Provincial Park is part of the Appalachian Mountains. Other significant peaks in the park include Mount Bailey, Bald Mountain, Mount Head, and the Sagamook.

Mount Carleton Provincial Park is home to more wildlife species than any other part of the province, and is also known for rare plants including Alpine blueberry and Bigelow's sedge. Hikers are sure to spot something of interest.

Currently there are 11 provincial parks in New Brunswick.

m
M

N's for the fishing Nets cast out with care,
hoping that shellfish and fish will be there.
There's lots to be found in the waters so blue
like salmon and oysters, and big lobster too!

Before the province was officially established, First Nations groups speared salmon and smoked fish. Today fisheries and aquaculture are a vital industry in the Gulf of St. Lawrence, the Northumberland Strait, and the Bay of Fundy. Over 50 species are harvested: lobster, snow crab, shrimp, scallops, oysters, salmon, herring, and trout.

Since New Brunswick waters hold a variety of species, there are many types of nets used. Gill nets are left overnight on the ocean floor, and are pulled to the surface in early morning. Other nets are dragged behind fishing boats in a funnel shape that traps fish. Salmon are raised in special cages with inner and outer nets, and lobsters are caught in net-covered baited traps.

Many communities celebrate the harvests with festivals. These include Shediac (lobster), Campbellton (salmon), Richibucto (scallop), Maisonnette (oyster), Bouctouche (mollusc), and Moncton (seafood).

William Eldon O'Ree of Fredericton crossed colour barriers as the first black player in the National Hockey League. In 1958 he signed with the Boston Bruins, playing parts of the 1957-58 and the 1960-61 seasons. He switched to the WHL, and led the league in goals (38) while playing for the LA Blades in 1964-65. Playing later for the American Hockey League, he scored 45 points in 50 games for the New Haven Nighthawks in their 1972-73 season.

O'Ree was appointed Director of the NHL's Youth Development/USA Hockey Diversity Task Force in 1998, and in 2003 he was awarded the Lester Patrick Award for outstanding service to hockey in the United States.

He made our province proud, and in 1984 he was inducted into the New Brunswick Sports Hall of Fame. He has since received awards in the United States, including the 2006 induction into the African-American Sports Hall of Fame.

In looking at athletes, an **O** there will be
in NHL team player Willie O'Ree.
His colour made history in NHL score.
He was the first black player—now there are more.

P p

P While harvesting crops from the New Brunswick soil
you'll find —Potatoes to bake, fry, or boil.
In baskets or bushels, or sold by the pound,
they're our biggest harvest that comes from the ground.

Potatoes are the biggest ground crop in New Brunswick. The province grows over 22,000 hectares of potatoes each year, and ships them to over 30 countries. New Brunswick has a unique soil type, named "Holmesville soil," which is one of the most fertile for growing potatoes. Many believe that the soil accounts for the desirable taste of the potatoes. The Shepody variety, used the world over, was developed in New Brunswick.

The McCain family had been exporting seed potatoes since 1914, and in 1956, brothers Harrison and Wallace McCain founded the McCain frozen food business in Florenceville. In 1957, under the name of McCain Foods, the production of frozen french fries began. Today McCain has production plants in Florenceville and Grand Falls, and in Prince Edward Island, Ontario, Quebec, Manitoba, and Alberta. If you plan to travel outside of Canada, you can buy McCain french fries in London, Paris, New York, Sydney, and Tel Aviv.

For more than 20 years an annual festival in Miramichi has celebrated the long and strong heritage of the Irish in New Brunswick. In addition to being surrounded by Irish music, dance, and lore, visitors can immerse themselves in rich Irish culture through workshops and special activities. Participants can try their hand at the tin whistle or Irish drum, learn a few steps of the jig or reel, practice a few Gaelic phrases, or enter the red hair contest. A stroll down the historic city walks reveals the stunning view of the Miramichi River, famous both for its scenery and the fabulous salmon fishing. As they say on the Miramichi: "Cead Mile Failte"— a hundred thousand welcomes!

If you enjoy cultural festivals, don't forget to also visit the New Brunswick Highland Games and Scottish Festival, held every July on the grounds of Old Government House in Fredericton.

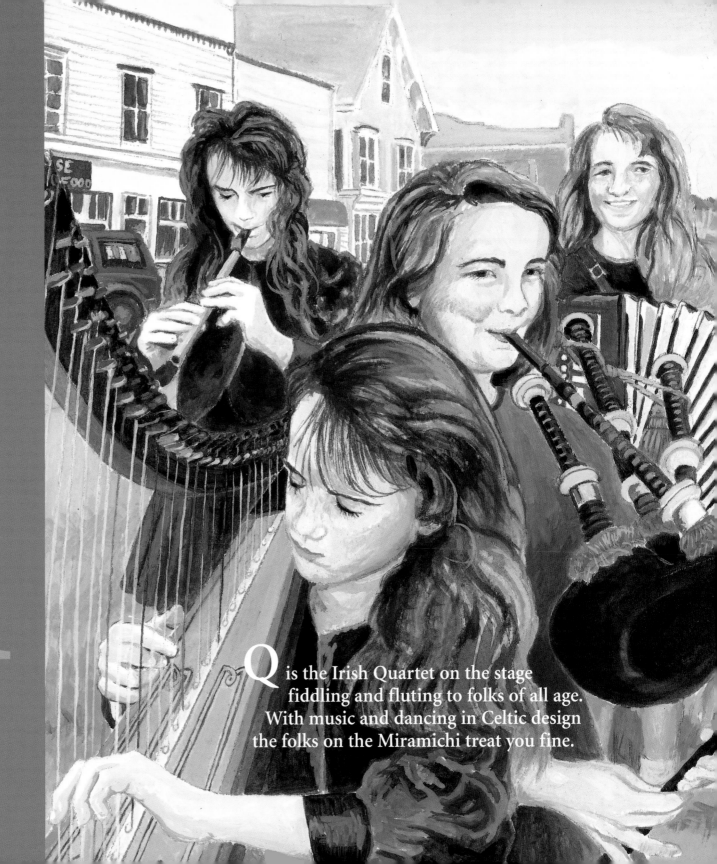

Q is the Irish Quartet on the stage
fiddling and fluting to folks of all age.
With music and dancing in Celtic design
the folks on the Miramichi treat you fine.

R r

R's for the mighty Saint John River flow
that helped early settlers move to and fro.
From green river valley the gentle hills roll;
a breathtaking view that will capture your soul.

The Saint John River, New Brunswick's longest river, is an impressive 673 kilometres long. It flows from northern Maine into New Brunswick and continues south through the province into the Bay of Fundy.

A fascinating phenomenon known as the Reversing Falls takes place in Saint John, where the river empties into the Bay of Fundy. When the tide is low, it empties into the bay through a narrow gorge. It passes an underwater ledge, thus creating a waterfall. As the bay tides begin to rise, they slow the course of the river and finally stop the river's flow completely. Shortly afterward the tides become higher than the level of the river, and the river slowly begins to run upstream. As the tides continue to rise, the reverse flow gradually increases and the waterfall begins to form in the opposite direction. This force is so powerful that it pushes back the water flowing to the sea, and for a short time twice each day, the river actually flows backward. It is felt as far upstream as Fredericton—over 100 kilometres away!

S is the Softwood of balsam fir trees,
waving their bright emerald boughs in the breeze.
They whisper a secret to dear Sister Sky
and listen as Brother Wind sends a reply.

In 1987 the balsam fir was named the official tree of New Brunswick. A beautiful, full softwood tree, it is one of the most popular Christmas trees on the market. It grows easily, and accounts for 97% of the province's Christmas tree industry. Trees are sold locally, and are exported to other parts of Canada and the U.S. The Boston Commons receives a large tree every year from the children of New Brunswick as thanks for Boston's help in the devastating Saint John fire of 1877.

About 80 to 85 percent of the province is covered by forest. In addition to the balsam fir, spruce, tamarack, cedar, hemlock, birch, and pine are common. Maple trees produce some of Canada's finest maple syrup. The forests are home to many species of wildlife including bears, deer, martens, moose, pheasants, rabbits, skunks, squirrels, woodcocks, and wildcats.

Forestry is one of the province's largest industries, employing close to 30,000 people. Forest products include lumber, plywood, and fuel, and pulp and paper mills are also dependent on them. New Brunswick is considered a leader in forest management.

Ss

T's for the Tides of the Fundy's wild coast.
The highest tides in the world we boast.
The rocks near the shoreline are far from just flat—
they're carved out by tidewaters—imagine that!

Tt

The tides in the Bay of Fundy, nestled between New Brunswick and Nova Scotia, are the highest and the wildest in the world. Twice daily the water rises to the exceptional height of up to 16 metres. Then it reverses and drains back out to sea, rushing in again when the tide turns. Fundy's onslaught of water, roughly every 12 hours and 30 minutes, is estimated to nearly equal the 24 hour flow of all the rivers in the world.

Hopewell Rocks are known as one of the marine wonders of the world. Fundy's mighty tides wash these shores twice daily, and sculpt the cliffs at Hopewell Cape into strange, rocky shapes that resemble giant flowerpots. These are transformed into little islands during high tide. Thousands of tourists come to visit the famous "flowerpot rocks" to experience the beauty and power of the Fundy tides. The 41 kilometre Fundy trail in St. Martins is another great place to explore the awesome rock carvings made by the tide.

U's Universities, aged and wise—
from humble beginnings they all came to rise.
In New Brunswick schools many fine firsts occurred,
for good was the deed, and proud was the word.

New Brunswick has at least 8 universities, including one where students take their classes online and don't even have to go to school!

Founded in 1785, the University of New Brunswick is the oldest English-language university in Canada, and is one of the oldest public universities in North America.

The first Canadian university to award a Bachelor of Fine Arts degree was Mount Allison University, in 1941. Famous instructors and directors included Lawren P. Harris, son of the Group of Seven member Lawren Harris, Alex Colville, and David Silverberg.

St. Thomas University had its beginnings in 1910 with the Basillian Fathers of Toronto. It became a degree-granting institution in 1934.

The L'Université de Moncton is Canada's largest francophone university outside of the province of Quebec. In addition to granting arts degrees, it offers programs in law, nursing, and forestry.

U u

V's for the Violet that grows wild and free
with petals of purple that wave lazily.
Although it's a small thing, it holds a great power
for this little plant is our provincial flower.

V
v

The purple violet was adopted as New Brunswick's flower on December 1, 1936, through a cooperative effort of New Brunswick's schoolchildren and the provincial Women's Institute. The plant generally grows between 12 and 25 centimetres tall with lush green leaves and purple flowers. Violets are generally thought of as spring flowers, but they can blossom up to early autumn. The flowers of the purple violet have been used in jams and syrups, and are believed to have some medicinal properties as well.

The black-capped chickadee was named the provincial bird in August of 1983 through a contest with the provincial Federation of Naturalists. This small and relatively tame backyard bird is distinctly patterned with a black cap and bib, and has white cheeks and a brownish body. The characteristic sound "chick-a-dee-dee" of the black-capped chickadee is one of the most complex vocalizations in the entire animal kingdom. With only slight variations they can contact other birds, warn of danger, look for a partner, or identify themselves to another flock.

You don't have to go to an aquarium to see some of the many species of whales. Boatloads of tourists leave the southern coast of New Brunswick to view the exceptional marine life. The rich feeding grounds in the Bay of Fundy make this area one of the most popular sites in the world for viewing marine mammals. Finback whales, the second largest in the world, are commonly seen, and the "blow" from their spout is impressively high. Humpback whales, with their bumpy flippers and knobby snouts, make occasional visits as well. Other whales that have been sighted in the Bay of Fundy include the minke, the North Atlantic right whale, the sei whale, and the (orca) killer whale. Dolphins and seal spottings are also common.

In Atlantic waters the W's for Whale
with extra-large fins and a powerful tail.
Though massive in size, they are graceful to see
as they jet from the water and splash in the sea.

The motto, Spem reduxit (Hope restored), symbolizes the haven for Loyalists who fled to New Brunswick after the American Revolution.

The motto is displayed on the coat of arms, which began when the shield (a golden lion and an ancient ship) and the motto were approved on May 26, 1868 by Queen Victoria. The ship, known as a galley, symbolized the Maritime location of the province, and the early shipbuilding industry. The lion linked to the arms of the Duchy of Brunswick in Germany, owned by King George III at the time. The province took its official name from this Duchy. The coat of arms was completed with a crest (a leaping atlantic salmon with St. Edward's crown), supporters (white-tailed deer with Maliseet collars), and a compartment (the violet and the fiddlehead).

The provincial flag was adopted on February 24, 1965. It portrays the golden lion and the ancient oared galley based on the same in the coat of arms.

An X can be found in our motto's wise words
Spem reduxit—for that means "hope restored."
Loyalist refugees came to our shore
escaping the harsh revolutionary war.

Yy

From Maliseet baskets to Acadian and Loyalist rugs, weaving has long been part of New Brunswick's history. Today students at the New Brunswick College of Craft and Design learn how to create decorative woven works.

Over the years countless weaving interest groups sprouted up in the province. Some of these are still thriving today. One of the most famous was the Madawaska Weavers of Saint-Leonard, who produced skirts, scarves, ties, and other fine items.

In honour of Fredericton's 200th birthday as the capital of New Brunswick (1985), two talented artists created a unique series of tapestries depicting the history of the city. The tapestries, designed by Mrs. Gertrude E. Duffie, were handwoven by Dr. Ivan Crowell, using yarn from the Briggs & Little mill in New Brunswick. The 27 brightly coloured tapestries portray the social and political history of Fredericton. They are believed to be the only series of woven tapestries in the world that depict the history of a city.

Y's for the Yarn as the shuttle makes room,
weft into warp on a grand weaving loom.
With colours majestic and patterns sublime
they narrate the story of New Brunswick's time.

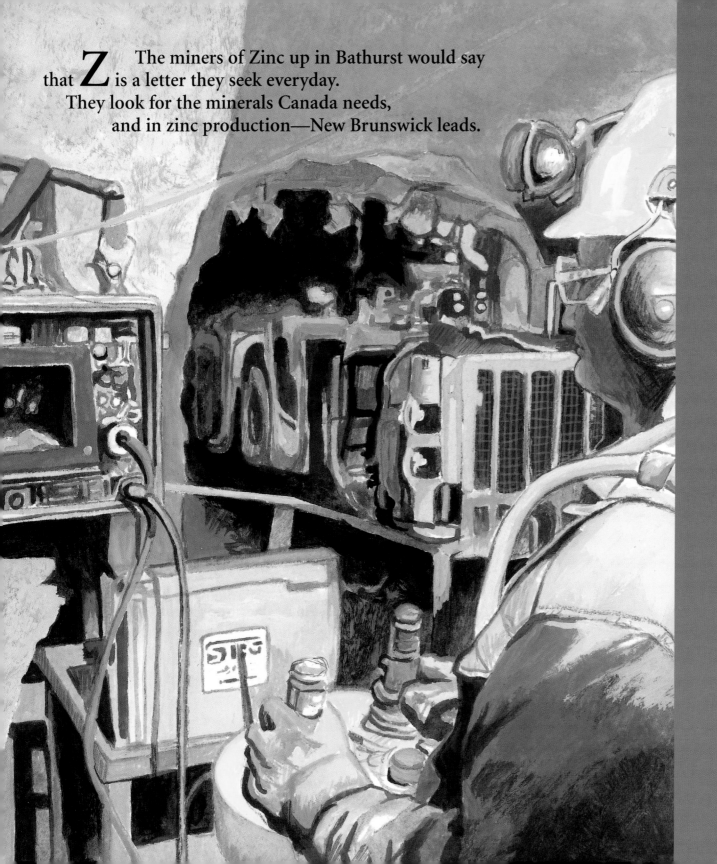

Z The miners of Zinc up in Bathurst would say
that **Z** is a letter they seek everyday.
They look for the minerals Canada needs,
and in zinc production—New Brunswick leads.

New Brunswick ranks first in Canada's output of zinc and lead, and is responsible for a significant share of Canada's mining resources. Base metals (zinc, silver, lead, copper, and some gold) make up about two-thirds of all minerals mined. At one time New Brunswick was the only Canadian producer of antimony, a mineral used in medicines, matches, and fireproofing materials. Another rare metal is bismuth, used in making metal alloys. New Brunswick is the source of about 70 percent of Canada's bismuth. Nonmetal mining includes marl, peat moss, potash, silica, salt, and sulphur. New Brunswick also mines fuels and structural materials such as lime, sand, and gravel.

Coast to Capital

1. What does the motto of New Brunswick mean?

2. What are the two major First Nations groups of New Brunswick?

3. Where is a popular site in New Brunswick to see finback whales?

4. Who was the first black hockey player in the NHL?

5. What is the longest river in New Brunswick?

6. What percentage of New Brunswick speaks French as a first language?

7. Where are the highest tides in the world found?

8. What are the names of New Brunswick's two national parks?

9. Where is the longest covered bridge in the world?

10. What percentage of New Brunswick is covered by forest?

11. What ocean snack is dried and eaten much like potato chips?

12. New Brunswick ranks first in Canada's output of what mined resource(s)?

13. How many species of fish and shellfish does New Brunswick harvest each year?

14. What is the provincial bird of New Brunswick?

15. What spring fern is a favourite green to eat?

16. Where was Canada's first Bachelor of Fine Arts degree awarded? When?

17. What was the first Canadian company to sell Valentine heart boxes filled with candies?

Answers

1. "Hope restored."

2. Mi'kmaq and Maliseet

3. The southern coast of New Brunswick (Bay of Fundy)

4. William (Willie) Eldon O'Ree

5. Saint John River

6. About 33%

7. Bay of Fundy

8. Kouchibouguac National Park
    Fundy National Park

9. Hartland, New Brunswick

10. About 80% to 85%

11. Dulse

12. Zinc (and lead)

13. Over 50

14. Black-capped chickadee

15. Fiddlehead

16. Mount Allison University, in 1941

17. Ganong

Marilyn Lohnes

Marilyn Lohnes knows, after living in New Brunswick for 11 years, it is a truly special province. She presently resides in the capital city, Fredericton. Marilyn has worked for many years as a professional librarian, has read thousands of stories to children, and helped to bring authors to New Brunswick through the Canadian Children's Book Week.

In her spare time she likes to explore the province with her husband, Richard. They pack a picnic lunch and kayak, hike, or simply drive to discover wonderful new places.

Susan Tooke

Born in New Jersey, Susan received her professional training from Virginia Commonwealth University, Richmond, Virginia and the New School in New York. She moved to Canada in 1980, and has made Halifax, Nova Scotia her home.

Susan has received the Lillian Shepherd Memorial Award for Excellence in Illustration, and the Mayor's Award for *Full Moon Rising*. Her work is consistently chosen by the Canadian Children's Book Centre as a starred selection for the Our Choice Award. In describing her artwork, Susan states: "I breathe real life into my images—the sounds, smells, colors, and idiosyncrasies of specific places and the people who inhabit them."